It was a beautiful day on Strawberry Street.
The sun warmed the air, the flowers smelled sweet.

The sky was bright blue, the wind was quite still.
It was quiet and peaceful and restful until...

1

"It's a mystery!" she says. "A case that we'll crack. Let's be detectives and get Carson back!"

"Let's retrace your steps like detectives do. You spent time with Grandma. Were you at the zoo?"

6

Readers, will you help us? Make a notation.
The pictures have clues to Carson's location.

Be a detective, a sleuth, and help solve the case.
Look for evidence, a hint, a tip or a trace.

7

We were in Ocean City enjoying the sights...
the boardwalk, the beach, the bright yellow kites,

the parks and the boats, the places to eat,
happy vacationers strolling the street.

We rode bikes on the boardwalk, relaxed in the sun,
then we played a few games. Boy, was that fun!

There was so much to do! We browsed through the shops.
Is Carson at the store where I bought new flip flops?

Is Carson at Dolles? Did he fall on the floor?
Did I drop him in taffy as I entered the store?

Is he covered in caramels in the candy display?
Or next to the fudge on a big silver tray?

Our next stop was the OC Life-Saving Station.
What a great place! A fun destination!

We learned about shipwrecks and surfboats and crews,
about mermaids, marine life and brave sea rescues.

Is Carson in a fish tank? Is he all alone?
Near the mermaid display? Or big shark jawbone?

We went to the beach, put on suntan lotion,
and went boogie boarding out in the ocean.

Did I drop Carson in the water? Or in the sand?
Is he sitting in a beach chair getting suntanned?

At Souvenir City, I bought a sea shell.
Is that where I left him? Is that where he fell?

Is he under a toy? Did he fall from my hand
near the hermit crab cage or big sunglass stand?

We stopped at Mug & Mallet for crabs and cold iced tea.
Did I drop Carson as I ate? Where, oh where, is he?

Is he on the table? Next to the fish fillet?
Buried in the clam strips? Or on the waiter's tray?

We drove to Berlin so that we could go hiking, kayaking, bird watching, shopping and biking!

At Cupcakes in Bloom we ate lots of sweet treats. Did I leave Carson there

on one of the seats?

Is he at Treasure Chest? Or Baked Dessert Café? Next to a diamond necklace? Or giant cookie tray?

Is Carson at the Comfort Suites? Is he in the pool?
Did I leave him in the gym? Or sitting on a stool?

Detective work is tricky. This case is hard to crack.
I need to find some clues. I must get Carson back!

Wockenfuss Candies was a super sweet stop.
They had licorice and gummis and crab lollipops!

Is Carson buried in truffles? Or next to the nuts?
Did I drop him somewhere?   At times, I'm a klutz!

Is my crab at Captain's Galley? Could that be the place?
Is that where I dropped Carson? We need to solve this case!

The mystery continues. Did he fall onto the floor?
Is he in the crabcakes? Or next to the front door?

We went to the Air Show and watched the jets fly.
They were fast! They were loud as they streaked through the sky.

A parachute team performed a brave stunt.
Did I drop Carson as I watched from the beachfront?

Phillips Seafood was filled with happy faces and bright smiles, cheerful diners everywhere, at tables and in aisles.

Is Carson in the kitchen? I really hope he's not.
The chef might think he's a real crab and toss him in a pot!

22

We stopped at Seaside Country Store to buy some licorice.

Is Carson in a candy bin next to the Swedish fish?

Is he on a shelf of toys or near the mango tea?
Did he fall into the fudge? Where could Carson be?

WHERE IS CARSON?!?

Readers, do you know where Carson might be?
Did you see the clue? It solves the mystery!

Did you look everywhere? Did you search every place?
Turn the page to find the answer! Let's crack this case!

24

Readers, thank you for your help!
You really saved the day!

The mystery is over.
Carson's back. Hooray!

26

To my Blummers...
you are my everything. - D.B.

Ty, Molly & Sean –
you make me laugh every day! - L.S.

"Be who you are and say what you want,
because those who mind don't matter and
those who matter don't mind." -Dr. Seuss

Other books by Mainstay Publishing...

Check www.mainstaypublishing.com for links to all featured destinations.